"Favor

and Allure.

Mignon

2005

Pearls from the Soul

*A collection of poems
with commentary*

WRITTEN BY MIGNON RENAE SPENCER

COVER PHOTOGRAPH BY PETE CASABONNE

GRAPHICS BY ZOILA TORRES

Scriptures cited and paraphrased from The Original Chain-Referenced Thompson
Study Bible, King James Version, World Bible Publishers, Inc., 1982.

Library of Congress Conrol No. 2005901544
ISBN 0-9763871-0-7

ACKNOWLEDGEMENTS

In memory of my mother, Macy V. Jones,

who said that I could

accomplish any thing, if I

tried hard enough.

To my husband, Clarence, for his love and support,

to my son, Dante, for his love and loyalty and

to Pastor Ellen Housley for her encouragement

to move ahead with the publishing of the book.

To Marie Goff, my friend and editor. You are an awesome and talented woman.

To Cynthia and Pete for your love, friendship and the wonderful photography.

To Zoila Torres, my friend and graphic artist extraordinaire.

And to all my friends and family who have been a source

of inspiration for this book.

I dedicate this book to the life and legacy of my grandmother, Susie Jones.

CONTENTS

Pearls from the Soul.. 2
The Elderly Lover.. 4
The Rain is Coming 6
Happy Father's Day 8
The Blessed Hope 10
When Two Shall Meet... 12
Lovers' Dance 14
Broken Engagement.. 16
First Deception... 18
The Marriage Supper 20
At the Pool of Bethsaida 22
A False Friend 24
Desperation 26
The Seasons of Love... 28
The Infidel.. 30
Baby Boomers.. 32
Stay on God's Path... 34
A Funny thing Happened at the Beach 36
Life... 38
Many are Called... 40
Withstand, You Can 42
Incarnate Again 44
Black Widow.. 46
Battle to Victory... 48
Just Be Me.. 50
The Empty Nest 52
The Suicidal Soul... 54
Slavery is in My Family History.. 56
The Curse 58
A Virtuous Woman of God.. 60
The King is Calling... 62
Someone Has to Pay 64
Women Admired 66
Pause from the World... 68
September 11, 2001: War on America 70
The God Child.. 72
The Prophetess 74
Hosanna, Hosanna... 76
The Ready Church 78
The Miracle Surgeon.. 80

FOREWORD

*T*hroughout life, a person experiences many things. From the birth of a dream to the elevation to a king. From the untimely death of a friend to the beginning of the end. This thing called life is a jagged, linear line of hype. It's full of ups, downs, bends, curves and turnarounds. You can take hold of it and live it. Or you can fall in a pit and decide to quit. And then profess that it is all vanity. Or even lose your sanity. But when the final bell tolls, a legacy of thee unfolds.

This book expresses in poetic form some of life's trials, tribulations, joys and sorrows. It contains poems with background stories. You'll laugh, you'll cry, you'll relate, you'll have peace, you'll be relieved to know that you did not travel the road called "life" alone.

Blessings & Favor,
Mignon Renae Spencer

BIOGRAPHY OF
M. RENAE JONES SPENCER

*M*ignon Renae Jones Spencer is the daughter of Claudie Bee Jones and the late Macy V. Jones of Morrow, Georgia. Renae was born March 29, 1957, at the Hugh Spalding Hospital in Atlanta and has six siblings, three brothers and three sisters.

She was an excellent student throughout her early school years, representing her school in a statewide spelling bee, was class president in the fifth grade, played the clarinet in the school band and was class valedictorian in the sixth grade.

Renae worked during her junior and senior school years, first in a peach orchard, fertilizing peach trees at fifty cents a day. Other jobs included a waitress, cleaning homes, summer camp leader and as a senior, repackaging returns in the warehouse of a major retailer.

An incident occurred after her fifth birthday, at summer day care, that was only her secret; however it traumatized her life. Early on she expressed her thoughts through poetry, writing since she was seven years old.

After passing the 11th grade, she became a young wife but continued study and graduated from a home study high school in 1975, at which time her son, Solomon Dante Baines, was born.

While working fulltime, she attended Georgia State University and received the B.A. in psychology. Later on, she pursued her studies for the M.A. in social science. Renae is the first child and grandchild in her family to earn a college degree, which was her childhood dream.

After high school, she worked as a sales associates, receptionist and product manager. She was training director for a local government for five years, where she "opened the doors" to the first employee university. She started her own business, BGU Associates, that has provided training and life coaching to public and private organizations.

Renae has appeared as guest poet of the week at the popular website, Poeticallyspeaking.com after submitting two of her favorite poems: "The Elderly Lover" and the "Virtuous Woman of God". As a result, she was invited to appear as guest poet on the XM Radio program The Spoken Word.

She married Clarence Spencer, in 1996. Her only child, Solomon Dante Baines, who served in the Armed Forces from 1994-98, is attending college to earn a bachelors degree in visual communication. The Spencers make their home in Hampton, Georgia.

Pearls From the Soul, Volume I, is her first published edition of poetry.

Pearls from the Soul

A pearl, like the human subconsciousness, is made by a living animal. It is made by a living shelled creature with a soft inside. A foreign object enters a mollusk and begins a swirling action that results in the formation of a beautiful pearl—and takes many years to develop. A distinctive feature of the pearl is that it glows from within—a lot like us. Someone deposited something into you. Some of it was good and some of it was bad. Nonetheless, it formed pearls in your soul.

*When was the last time you shared
one of your good pearls?*

PEARLS FROM THE SOUL

A small particle of a wind beaten life
Made from laughter, sorrows and strife
Spiraling and growing in the sea of calm
Revealing a most beautiful and solid form.

Deep inside the core of a glowing pearl
A fortress built outside the ivory swirls
Every life experience deeply etched
In a soul that was vacuous and vexed

A sanctuary of peace, kindness and love
Virtues derived from being judged
An opened soul releases its sealed pearls
To unashamedly share with a waiting world.

ELDERLY LOVER

Everybody called her Luela Bell. She was 79 years old and lived on a $500 monthly social security check. She was a beautiful woman for her age. She had pretty cinnamon toned skin that had maintained its youthfulness. While she was overweight, she was generally happy and independent. She loved to cook and eat as you could imagine. During one visit, Luela Bell was glowing and she had some very exciting news for me. She told me that she was getting married. I was extremely happy for her. I inquired of the name of this fortunate, elderly gentleman. Of course, she indicated that I was a bit on the nosey side. Well I pressed her. She said I could not tell anyone. I agreed. She said her suitor was Forrest. Well I tried to keep my mouth closed. It was such shocking news. I'm thinking to myself... he's only 39 years old. He's young enough to be your great grandson. Well I restrained myself. I realized that she was happy. Forrest made her happy. They had been "dating" for about 11 years. She was in love. She showed me all the expensive gifts he had purchased for her. It was an honor to keep her secret.

Age has nothing to do with love.

ELDERLY LOVER

She was seventy-nine
He was young and kind
No one knew her secret lover
Was a mere thirty-nine.

He courted her many hours
Through winter snow and April showers
An odd intimacy of great power
A love likened to a strong tower.

Dreams of a wedding day
Of which no one could say
A heavy love for the balance to weigh
In her mind a wedding dress would stay.

Sickness soon knocked at her door
Her weight crumbled weak legs to the floor
She couldn't live in her home anymore
Sadness would not leave either soul's shore.

Joy left her ancient, fragrant bed
He wasn't there to rub her graying head
By deep bereavement she was led
To daily thoughts of being dead.

Life was empty without her young love
So one day she smiled and took flight above
Standing at her grave his tears he rubbed
His lover had gone to heaven's sweet cove.

I THE RAIN IS COMING

grew up in rural Georgia. The house in which I grew up was on a couple of acres and had red and green apple trees, walnut trees, persimmon, peach and pear trees. Summers at the house on Highway 138 were the best of my life. During those days, my grandmother, who lived with my family for many years, washed our clothes using the old wringer-type washing machine and hung the wet clothes outside on the clothesline to dry. We didn't need fabric softener and fresheners. The sun and the summer breeze were better than any Downy. I will never forget how my brother Tony and I would play together in the woods and in the small stream that flowed through the field in the back of our house. When it would rain, Grandma would yell for us to come in from the rain. My best and most soothing childhood memory is the sound of the rain falling on the hot, tin roof.

Memories of the past can soothe your soul.

THE RAIN IS COMING

Sprawled on a large rock in a grassy field

The sunshine drapes my shoulders

The smell of summer in the air

Leaning back on my skinny elbows

The sun beams upon my ebony face

As I talk to God

My brother interrupts His quiet voice

Whispering among the grasses

His brown skin ashened from the sand

He thinks today is for catching tadpoles

We run toward the stream

Anxious to feel the cool waters upon our skin

We love the stream

Its crystal water points us to the tadpoles

Grandma calls

We run back to the house

The clouds shield us from the sun

A persimmon tree moves toward us

Its fruit small and orange, its thirsty leaves

A white apron in the distance

Heaven opens her windows

In the nearby woods, the leaves dance

We see grandma

Her shining smile and silver hair

She reaches for the clothesline

We feel God's rain.

HAPPY FATHER'S DAY

One day I realized that my Mother had always been the center of my attention. She was the one who spent the greatest amount of time with my six siblings and me. She played with us, she talked with us, and she took us shopping and bought us things. She was the one who sent one of us to get the child who would run when it was time for a whipping. She was even the one who made you go get your own "switch," when you required corporal punishment. She baked our favorite cakes at Christmas time. Mom taught us to drive a car. She never knew it, but when I was a little girl, she was the apple of my eye. She was the air that I breathed. I knew that I wanted to die first, because I couldn't live without her. Well, my mother died first. I could adjust to life without her because I was older and my Dad was here. One day I realized how much my dad meant to me and I told him with a framed poem on Father's Day. What a wonderful father he is!

*Remember to let Dad know
that you love him, too!*

HAPPY FATHER'S DAY

Daddy, we love you.
You have given much to what we are today
You could have left us, as some dads. You
Stayed regardless of any difficulty of raising us.
You vowed to stay.

You were quiet, yet stern and chastened us because of
your love for us. We now understand that concept,
since our heavenly Father chastens us now.

We may never tell you that we love you, or find
Many occasions to show it, but we do. A love that
Has grown since we sat upon your knee.
We hope that you are as proud to be our father
As we are to be your children. Happy Fathers Day Dad!

THE BLESSED HOPE

*E*very human being reaches the time in life when you realize that you are not immortal. You discover that you will not live forever. You suddenly realize that you are going to die some day. You may be killed in an accident, die from a disease, or God forbid, at the hands of someone else. Nonetheless, you are going to leave this earth. You finally decide that you must know why you were born. Surely there is a reason that you came here. I decided that God created me and I came here to serve Him using the gifts and callings that He placed within me. My blessed hope is to stand before the throne someday for my final grade.

Build your hope on things eternal.

THE BLESSED HOPE

Who controls that old balance in life?
Why does pain cut like a knife?

Happiness comes, happiness goes.
Close your eyes; you are many years old.

The years before
Where did they go?

The passage of time
First life, then dying.

Time can heal the broken hearted
The rapture comes and the good depart.

WHEN TWO SHALL MEET

Every now and then you meet someone of the opposite sex of whom you are fond. Of course, he or she becomes enamored with you and wants more. However, you're only looking for a friend. You don't want to hurt anyone's feelings. Therefore, you gently attempt to explain that God is sovereign and that He orchestrates every area of life. As a result nothing can happen in life by chance. It is not always evident the reasons that people cross our paths, but God knows. He set it up.

Nothing happens by chance but by design.

WHEN TWO SHALL MEET

He knitted two hearts together
For a short season or maybe forever.

Only He knew the reason for the bond.
Would it result in someone being won?

Events in a Christian's life do not occur by chance
It's due to an orchestration of the master's hand.

Hear the silent word of the Lord.
Watch and pray. Be always on guard.

Saints paths do not cross for naught.
Their crossings might enhance the salt.

The string in the master knitter's needle
Sows love and hope to His hurting people.

LOVERS' DANCE

I will always remember the first time I met my spouse. He was a blind date. Our friends, who were dating each other at the time, decided that he and I would make a great couple. They were right. I thought he was the most wonderful person that I had ever met. His eyes had a light in them. He was warm, talkative, and quite charming. We were both shy; yet we were still able to discuss all the things we hated about dating and going to night clubs—which is where our friends took us after dinner. We didn't like the nightclub life and have never been back to one. Nonetheless, we've talked to each other every day since first meeting.

Sometimes love really does happen at the first bite.

LOVERS' DANCE

Coy, compassionate and quite kind
Perhaps, too, from love once blind.

Like a cloud, passion filled the space
Love had indelibly left its trace.

The conversation was just right;
Neither wanted to say good night.

A peck on the cheek; a wave of goodbye.
Through the night, no sleep for the eye.

Morning light brings a day of joy;
A beginning waltz for a girl and boy.

BROKEN ENGAGEMENT

There's nothing like a broken heart. You can't eat. You can't sleep. You don't want to go to bed at night. You don't want to get up in the morning. You feel like you're absolutely going to die or otherwise lose your mind. You can't stop thinking about the person. You wonder what you did wrong. It depresses you to see other couples together. You begrudge them their time of happiness. You cry because the radio keeps playing your same old, sad song. Then, when you get over it, you're embarrassed.

"Weeping endures for a night.
Joy comes in the morning."

BROKEN ENGAGEMENT

Silent suffering

Craving your mere presence

Wanting to inhale your scent

Will I see you again?

Will we kiss once more?

Pain tugs at my heart

Trying to break it

Yesterday the memory of you

Tomorrow perhaps a chance

To peer through the

Window of your soul and ask why.

First Deception

I remember how devastated I felt the first time I perceived that I had been deceived. Now, I am not the type to be deceptive. You can take me mostly at face value. I was really naive and thought others were as open and candid as I am. If someone told me something, I believed it. Because if I told you something, you could pretty well take it to the bank. A person that I loved and trusted with my life once abandoned every promise that had been made to me. Now, I'm more "street-wise," and I know that people will deceive you—sometimes intentionally and sometimes not. They will also smile in your face and talk about you behind your back. They will tell you they love you and at the same time confess undying love for someone else. I learned that "hurting people" hurt people.

Look beyond a fault. You might see a need.

FIRST DECEPTION

I see what blinded me yesterday
Love is blind, they say.
I pretended to see only the good.
I'm awake. I have my sight.
Oh, what a mare of a night!

Lies, deceit
Is it right?
Pain, despair
Nothing is really different.
Today is yesterday, isn't it?

Only I changed.
My blindness was replaced by pain.

I THE MARRIAGE SUPPER

was at the hospital the day my Mother passed away. She'd been in the hospital for several weeks. I somehow knew that this time she would not come out of the hospital. That particular day, I had packed a lunch because I planned to spend the day with her. When I arrived that morning, her breathing was fairly labored and she was not completely conscious. I had read that when a person begins to have a labored breathing pattern, the skin mottles, they start seeing or talking to people who have passed, it's close to their time. These are signs that the major organs are shutting down. I knew she was dying, but I was in denial at the same time. When she took her last breath, the spirit made a roaring sound as it left her body. I will never forget that experience.

There is no need to fear the passing of a loved one.

THE MARRIAGE SUPPER

In the year my Momma died,
I saw the Lord.
Eyes walled back toward heaven.
Fingernails turned to midnight.
Doctors walking away.
Saying it was over.

God was calling her
Thrashing upon the deathbed
The death pains in rapid succession
By her side stood the beating hearts
Of her own flesh and blood.
One singing a psalm.
One wiping her brow.
One praying for God to heal her.
One sitting quietly by her bedside.
One knowing her time was short.
One weeping for Momma and self.
Her favorite kissing her goodbye daily.

Another trumpet of God sounded
Each day she traveled from earth to heaven
Perhaps seeing many who had gone before,
Beckoning her from across the mysterious gulf.
One more visitor and Momma could go to sleep.

Her breathing changed.
Her eyes stretched wide in awesomeness.
I believe she could see the holy city as
The spirit left its earthen temple.

The magnificent glory cloud filled the room
The groom had come for his bride
He came just to escort Momma back.
A sound of wind parted her full lips
Her body stilled. She was at peace.
The ceremony ended. The groom had kissed
The bride. Tears of joy and sadness
Rolled down my cheeks upon her wedding gown.

I AT THE POOL OF BETHSAIDA

attended a three-day prayer retreat at Emory University's Candler School of Theology. It was held in the Georgia Mountains. The place was quiet and serene and nestled in the woods. It was the perfect location for a prayer retreat. I spent three days with female Methodist preachers, alumni of Candler. It was a very spiritual experience. This poem resulted from one of the activities.

There's nothing like getting away to pray.

At the Pool of Bethsaida

The pain is intense. I'm without strength.

They said she came yesterday.

She comes each day to stir the water,

The holy angel of God.

I'm here each day, too.

I've seen the others healed and leaping from

Bethsaida with joy.

It's my turn.

I see the rippling, swirling water.

Get out of the way.

Let me get in. Again I couldn't.

Today He came and asked a

simple question. Then He commanded

me to "take up my bed and walk."

And I did.

A FALSE FRIEND

A false friend can be male or female. How do we identify these individuals whom we allow to enter the sanctuary of our lives? I'm not sure you can always tell. However, if they come bearing no fruit, you can ascertain that they are not true friends. Here are some of the fruit I look for now: Available in time of need, positive and encouraging; give as much as they take, not showing jealousy of successes or accomplishments, not speaking ill of others (this type will talk about you, too) and when you've had a major surgery, a baby, or other major life crises, your true friends call or come by to ask if there's anything they can do to help. Now that's a true friend.

"A friend loves at all times."

A FALSE FRIEND

She speaks lies
Putting truth aside.

Saying, "I'll be there."
But is found nowhere.

She's self-centered
Her soul cannot be entered.

On you she leans
When you have a limp,
She's unseen.

She has no plan.
She deals with a slack hand.

Trust and lean only on God.
Eternal reliance He imparts.

He's a true friend until the end.

DESPERATION

A close friend of mine got involved in a relationship that was not good for her. She had been recently hurt in a previous relationship and was on the rebound. She was desperate to begin a new relationship because she could not bear to be alone. Her attempt to rebound boomeranged. She became involved with a man who was not able to love her. He had never received unconditional love and he was not able to give it. He had no real interest in a relationship. He was simply excited about the pursuit — the excitement of the unknown. Needless to say that she was devastated and is still getting over this experience.

Until you love God, you probably can't love others.

DESPERATION

Lonely eyes
Scanning the crowd
With beating hearts
In search
Of a home.

The flavor of pelt
The smell of passion
A lingering stare
From eyes that conceal.

THE SEASONS OF LOVE

*L*ove has seasons. You fall in and out. The first time your "forever love" wanes, you think your world has come to an end. However, if you hang in there, work on it a little, you see the fire ignite again. Too many people get divorced when they think the fire has gone out. They just need to throw a little lighter fluid on it. It restarts every time.

Love waxes and wanes. That's life. So let's grow up.

THE SEASONS OF LOVE

Once upon a time
Love was in the air
We were without care

Moments spent
For love was there
We were content

Once time apart was unbearable
Because love was there
Now it is bearable for loss of care.

Where is the love we
Said would never die
Were we just living a lie?

Can we return to days of sun?
Let's again have fun.

Is our love like the tree
That bends and breaks from
The heavy rain?
Or will we endure
And love once again?

The "Infidel"

The bible reads that a man who doesn't take care of his children is worse than an infidel. I say a man or woman that is not faithful in his or her relationship is an infidel. He or she is unfaithful. As a student of psychotherapy, I read about a woman who was cheating on her husband. She said that he did not suspect that she was unfaithful because he trusted her. Now you understand how someone in which you're dating or married has difficulty with trust.

"... in God have I put my trust; I will not fear what flesh can do unto me."

Psalm 56:4

The "Infidel"

He lives two lives.
Beware of his jive.

While with one he eats
And another he sleeps.

He's a little boy by name.
Can't seem to play a real man's game.

You fall in love with him.
And think he's a gem until you
Find lipstick on his cuffs or hem.

When will he realize the pain he brings?
And stop terrorizing God's feminine things.

For this man, salvation is needed.
Only when the voice of God is heeded.

When he has destroyed all the esteem that he can,
He'll fall to one knee and beg for the Master's hand.

BABY BOOMERS
1946-1964

Were you born between 1946 and 1964? If yes, you are a baby boomer. During these years, more infants were born than at any other time in the history of the United States. Nothing was given to us on a silver platter. We worked hard for everything we've earned—our education, our homes, our American dream. We worked so hard that when our children came along, we wanted to make it easier for them. So what did we do? We gave them everything. Was that a mistake?

After the Baby Boomers came the Generation X.

BABY BOOMERS

Homework, cooking and care taking.

Mother is a child.

They don't worry.

Mother is unhappy.

He serenades other women.

Mother is not well today.

Act older than five.

Check on the baby.

Iron father's work clothes.

Whip sister.

Brother needs to use the potty.

The mate was a child, too.

Parents without a partner.

A troubled child.

They say he's doing fine.

She needed him.

He needed her.

Mother wasn't there.

She was frightened.

Mother! I can't take care of myself.

STAY ON GOD'S PATH

S ometimes life's circumstances are so painful. You must speak to and encourage yourself. You have to realize that there is a great plan for your life. There will be pain and there will be sorrow. There will be those who will deceive you. There will be those who will not understand you and misinterpret your actions. Jesus, who was the greatest to walk among us, was called a devil. How could any of us expect to be treated better than Jesus was treated?

"And we know that all things work together for good to them that love God, to them who are called according to his purpose."

Stay on God's Path

"Let it go" they say.
You try day to day.

Engulfed by pain.
No empathy, how insane!

Man's goings are of the Lord.
A man can never know his own way.

Has life dealt this "bad hand"?
Some would give up and live off the land.

See His plan and you will stand.
Walk His way; have joy today.

Push not against the fierce wind.
And it will quickly come to an end.

Don't pause or stop to ask.
Just stay on God's unerring path.

A FUNNY THING HAPPENED
AT THE BEACH

At age 16, I experienced my most embarrassing yet funny moment. I went to the beach. It was the first and last time I would every wear a string bikini. By the time I got the nerve to take off my cover-up and go into the water, I splashed around in the deep so no one could see me in my suit. When I was returning to the shore, I noticed everyone staring at me. Well in my vanity, I began to twist my hips because they were admiring this sexy babe. Then suddenly, while all eyes were on me, a male classmate called to me and asked me to look down. To my chagrin, my "string top" was down around my waist. Needless to say, I wanted to shrink down to a grain of sand and get lost on the beach. I was sooo! embarrassed. A few years ago I told a friend this story. She laughed until she cried. I finally realized how funny it was and I laughed, too.

Take time to recall your most-embarrassing moment— now laugh!! (By the way, I never put on another two- piece swim suit.)

A Funny Thing Happened
at the Beach

That first red, string bikini
Hugged every chocolate mound
Of those ebony, strong curves
Sensual, steamy and round.
A 16-year-old with nerve!

Playing in the cool waters
Having fun with every wave
Those curvaceous, round hips
Oh what a sexy, hot babe!

Strolling sexily across the beach
Young and old admiring her
Snickering and staring at
What this chick was wearing!

"Look down" a friend said
A surprise awaits you below
That top wet and red
Is exposing a "twin peak" show!

She ran as fast as her feet would go
Hiding her tight, reddened face
From the applause of her show
To once again find poise and grace.

LIFE

*L*eo Tolstory once said that "the only significance of life consists in helping to establish the kingdom of God; and this can be done only by means of the acknowledgement and profession of the truth by each one of us."

Spend your life doing something that will outlast it.

LIFE

Who controls the balances of life?
Happiness comes and happiness goes.
Growing pains are stabs from a dull knife.
In a passing moment, you're old.
You can't capture time in your hand.
Life is sometimes filled with woes
And intermissions of spring rain and sand.
Followed by cold, Monday morning snows
That drape the day and arise with the sun.

Many Are Called

God is calling every believer. You may not be an apostle, prophet, pastor, evangelist, preacher or deacon. You may be a doctor, lawyer, housewife or construction worker or bank teller. You may be a singer, musician or orchestra leader. He has no respect of person, position or title. He simply desires to use every gift and every calling to minister to the world.

The field is white for harvest, but the laborers are few.

Many Are Called

From the womb I gave your name.
My wondrous destiny to your fame.

The very hairs on your head I numbered.
Know that my yoke will not encumber.

For you, I chose the refiner's fire.
You will reap, if you do not tire.

See my face in your reflection
Feel my soft nudge of election.

Withstand, You Can

A woman came to work on a temporary assignment in my office. We struck up a conversation and started talking about church and our belief in God. Well, she and her husband were ministers and had started a new church. I was a new Christian and was looking for a new church home. I was persuaded to visit her church—and later joined. She enticed me with a position as leader of the Singles Ministry. To make a long story short, the relationship between she and I didn't last. Our ministry was failing because it was built on lies and deception. She asked my opinion of what I thought was happening. Well she didn't like my answer. She became wrought with rage and jealousy, which she acted out. Needless to say, I was very hurt and left the church. She later called to ask for forgiveness for her actions. She had discovered that I was sent to serve her and she didn't recognize that until I left. (By the way, later on, I ran into her husband, she had divorced him and their ministry had ended.)

*"Beware how you treat strangers, as you may
be entertaining angels unawares."
(Also, you don't miss your water until your well is dry.)*

WITHSTAND, I CAN

How could it be?
This situation seems too great for me.

Hear my heart's cry for the learning list?
If I am still, the answer won't be missed.

Is this a fiery dart I don't want to touch?
I must persevere if the situation is such.

Will I survive this brief, grievous season, too?
If this is your chastening hand, you'll see me through.

Does this situation demand more of your hand?
I want to understand and I desire to follow your plan.

What would Jesus have done?
Your answer: "Humility my son."

Is it you who orders the steps of a good man?
If so, I must and I can withstand.

INCARNATE AGAIN

What is reincarnation all about it? Some people believe in it while others do not. Which of us can say that God does not recycle spirits? When a spirit leaves the body through death, why can't God send it back if He wants to? This is one topic I really look forward to discussing when I get to heaven because the holy scripture however reads that we die once and we're judged.

What is the origin of this theory?

INCARNATE AGAIN

She was a gent of maiden form
And he was a lass when men were men
They loved each other
Once upon a time as siblings.

They roamed the golden meadow
The daisy pollen tickling their noses
The warm sun through the trees dries
Their misty foreheads as they carve
Love stories on its wooden belly.

Their lives like storms, calm seas, and hurricanes
The trumpet sounds the call home
Death's sad sting and the spirits return
Bidding goodbye, they rush to their giver
Drawn to a place above the sky.

Regeneration, a different time and place
Familiar eyes meet in an odd way, in a
Strange land, pulled by a mysterious force.
Incarnate again. Time, again, brings
Haunting familiarity.

BLACK WIDOW

When I was a teenager, I fell head-over-heels in love. My boyfriend started to ignore me and no longer had time for me. I thought he was he was dating someone else. Well, he wouldn't tell me. So I decided the best way to know was to find out. I put on a disguise, borrowed a friend's car and followed him. Needless to say, my suspicions were correct. I cannot describe the emotional pain I felt. Looking back, my advice to you is this: When you're trying to catch a butterfly, just turn your back and it will come and light on your shoulder. If it doesn't, hunt it down and kill it. Just kidding.

"If you love something set it free, if it's yours, it will return to you."

BLACK WIDOW

She followed and lost him on the road.
Sometimes a heart of love
Has to bear a great load.
She denied what her heart had seen.
Not him, not her Mr. Clean.
Suspicion arose and
An investigation began.
She ceased her probe
You see, this was her man.

One day thinking him to be
Lonely for her love,
She decided on a visit
By direction from above.
Once inside the house to her
Wandering eye appeared
A folded envelope with
Red lipstick smeared.

She was crushed
And felt great despair.
She had to find the truth,
She didn't care.
She recalled a friend from long ago,
Grabbed the phone book
She had to know.

Finding the place
Was easy.
Seeing his car
Made her feel queasy.
Black Widow was her name.
She had spun a web and
Ensnared her game.

BATTLE TO VICTORY

A world-renown ministry experienced a terrible scandal in 1990. The media had a hey day with them. This quote by Robert Boyd Munger is a message to the media: "The church is not to be judged by the frailties or failures of its members. The church is to be judged for what it can do for a person, and what it offers in its ideals, its resources..."

The church is the salt of the earth.

BATTLE TO VICTORY

In a form of Lucifer
They come grinning, skinning
Wanting to know what is unknown
Slyly searching, probing
Digging into you to find
A flaw, a weakness, dirt

You refuse to indulge
Their attempts to excavate
Your life before the world
With their plastic smiles
Stretched over evil-colored enamel

Eventually they fantasize the unknown
And create lies, gossip and
All manner of evil thought against you
Ignoring them, you turn the other cheek
To find that they leave you for a season

Your ministry of love gains respect
It births and grows happiness for others
Men seek your counsel
For comfort, for answers, for peace

Alas, the devil raises his ugly head
This time you square your shoulders
And prepare for battle

Hesitantly, you ask God to
Put the sword to the throat
Of the enemy and see his hand
Move to vindicate you

Like David, you help God
Finding the best stone and sling
To bring Goliath down
No weapon formed against you can prosper
With might, you slay the giant

In your hand, you hold the gory victory prize
Men watch while you feel the power
Maliciousness, jealousy and deviousness
Run down your hand
The battle is over
Victory is finally yours
Goliath is dead
Dead for a season.

JUST BE ME

*N*obody can beat you being you, according to Bishop T.D. Jakes, one of America's favorite pastors. Don't compare yourself to other people. You have a unique set of gifts and talents that the world needs. No one can accomplish what you were born to do. It may appear that people want you to change and to be something else. Well, learn how to "chew up the straw and spit out the sticks." Take their useful advice and throw out the rest. Remember that people judge from the outward appearance. If you are an introvert, you can't become an extrovert. Be true to who you are.

> *"To thine own self be true."*
> Shakespeare

JUST BE ME

Let me out!

Cries the voice inside.

Are you miserable when I hide?

Relax and just be me, then you'll know

The real meaning of free.

Toss the façade and be what you are.

Without it, you will be happier by far.

If you're not what others think you should be.

They have the problem.

As for you, just be me.

THE EMPTY NEST

*E*very woman who has children looks forward to the time when her children will grow up, become independent and move away from home. Many mothers have experienced teenagers who decide to live with the absent father or a grandmother. No one knows the grief that is felt by the mother whose child suddenly leaves the nest after 17 or 18 years.

Show some love to a Mother whose child leaves her home before the appointed time.

The Empty Nest

Sitting in a lonely place that was once filled
With sound, presence and laughter
Replaced now by music and the faint feel of pain.

And God, where is He now?
I can't feel his presence
Only my own wretched existence
Living, mothering and working in a world
That does not accept its own.

The joy of the Lord would be my strength.
But I feel weak
To die would be gain.

I wish that God had not given free will.
He could then make choices for me.
I could lie down in green pastures
And feel no evil, no pain.

Joy will come in the morning.
Nights have passed since the last dawn.
I welcome death as my companion.
No more tears, no more sleepless nights.
No more pain.

THE SUICIDAL SOUL

*Z*ack worked for me. He was an extremely intelligent man who had become physically ill. He probably should have taken early retirement. However, the company, for whatever reason, did not take this action. They hired me to replace him and then changed his reporting relationship to me. This was an extremely challenging situation for both Zack and me. To be fair to him, I immediately assessed his gifts and abilities and created a new position to reduce his stress, as well as, to make the use of the skills he brought to the team. Unknown to me, Zack had attempted six times to kill himself. One morning, he went about his way to do his job as usual. None of us knew that he had a plan for that day. He finished his morning task, went to purchase a shotgun, called up EMS and pulled the trigger. I was devastated when I learned what Zack had done. However, instead of a suicide note, he left a greeting card for me on his desk.

Be kind to your employees, you never know what they've been through. (Due to privacy law, the Human Resources folk can't tell you.)

THE SUICIDAL SOUL

The lies behind his brown Hemingway eyes
Concealed his sadness, his weariness, his pride
He couldn't show who he was
Fearing rejection, this man of nods.

His tiny autograph reflected the smallness inside
Shuffling when walking with a struggling stride.
There was no title on the cover of his book.
You made much effort just to get a quick look.

With a cigarette in hand, he had a blank stare.
His insides shouted that the world didn't care.
The computer God gave him had a common crash.
He clicked but he couldn't open his Freud, Jung or Plath.

All alone by himself, he turned off the light.
No one saw his warm tears at night.
One April day, he decided not to stay.
He did his job as usual and went on his way.

He wrote them a note and put away the cat.
He made a phone call and that was that!
They heard sirens but EMS was too late.
He was gone from a body once loved with hate.

His note read, "Good bye Mom, Julie and Jerri.
Please cremate me. I won't like the cemetery.
So scatter my ashes and please don't cry."
They'll forget me as time goes by.

Zack's soul went to a place, that's above or below.
His painful flesh troubling him no more.
He decided he had to vacate his space.
Leaving someone else to finish his race.

SLAVERY IS IN
MY FAMILY HISTORY

A close friend asked me: "Why do Black people keep talking about slavery? Something that happened a thousand years ago. Well, 138 years ago, Abraham Lincoln signed the Emancipation Proclamation that set the slaves free. My great, great, grandmother was a slave. This is our history. We have to talk about it.

He who forgets the past is certain to repeat it.
Unknown

SLAVERY IS IN MY FAMILY HISTORY

Assembled for auction from bids high and low
Sold to John L. Jones, the English banker
Landlord and guardian of our grandfather's soul
Four hundred years, then the 1865 promise
That set captives free and the hope of 40 acres
And a mule most would never see.

Grandpa was born 1904, son of a man from the ivory shore
Snatched, pulled from a place where men
Were free to do and to be. His tales of serfdom
Evoke laughter, tears, and rage
About a history that should not be denied any race or age.

Expressionless, he talks of the past.
The pain, bloodshed, hunger, raping of aunts
Daughters and young cousins. Each night a different
Shade of bed warmer. Master did not care that he harmed them.

The amazing strength of his humble soul inherited
From the genes of shotgun humility. Hardly anyone speaks
Of the silent lamentation of his bloodline.

Grandpa wears a peace most cannot comprehend
For he lived to see his Moses parting the red sea with a movement
That reached shore to shore. Rejoicing upon wobbly knees once strong,
He shouts, Free at last! Free at last!

Thank God almighty; we're free from history that's past.

THE CURSE

*W*hat is a dramatic monologue? "The Curse" is an example of a dramatic monologue. It's a poetic form that speaks in the voice of someone else or an animal or thing. Ever wondered how God really felt about the happenings in the Garden?

I believe in Creationalism. How about you?

THE CURSE

I made Adam and Eve in my likeness
Conceived them in my garden
Provided a table of pomegranate, nuts and fruit
Created clear streams of water to satisfy their thirst
My animal kingdom and everything that swam
In the sea, my creation named and had dominion over.

I walked and talked with Adam in the cool of day
Listening to his concerns.

They were restless.
I instructed them about good and evil.
I so desperately wanted to keep evil from them.
I watched them that day.
Their human ignorance veiled my omnipresence.
I fought back despair as they reached in the leaves.
A reach that would change the destiny of the human race.
That fruit was the only thing I withheld from them.
A small fruit—to test their obedience.

I watched them cover their nakedness.
I lost them in my anger that day.
In pain, they would fill the earth.
In toil that would build their world.
I chased their corruption from my garden.
A cherub now guards the entranceway.

M A VIRTUOUS WOMAN OF GOD

aya Angelou, my favorite poet, inspired me to tell of the virtuous woman in Proverbs 31 in the Old Testament of the bible.

What a woman!

A Virtuous Woman of God

Women are curious of the confidence that she holds
She's not a Marilyn Monroe nor built like Jackie O'
She's a virtuous woman, whose jewels are
A trusting husband
With no need of spoil.
Strong hands that
Anoint the sick with oil.
A shrewd spirit man
Who can purchase land.
She's a woman you see.
A virtuous woman of God.

When she enters a stage
Her image reflects her age
Her mouth opens with wisdom.
For her life is the kingdom.
Her house is not a mess.
And her children call her blessed.
Beauty is only vain.
The fear of the Lord is her aim.
She's a woman you see.
A virtuous woman of God.

People wonder what it is in her they see.
You see less of Jezebel and more of Naomi.
She tries to tell them but they don't understand.
It's the blessed hope
The agape in her heart
The fruit of the spirit
And the favor of God
She's His woman you see.
A virtuous woman of God.

THE KING IS CALLING

*J*esus said: " I am way, the truth and the life: no man cometh unto the Father, but by me."

"For God so loved the world, that he gave his only begotten Son that whosoever believeth in him should not perish, but have everlasting life." John 3:16

The King is Calling

For millenniums,
They offered tender lambs
In place of transgressions.

Then God sent Him.
The only one worthy to be the sacrifice.
As a dishonored soldier, He was stripped.

He drank a bitter cup.
He was humanity and divinity.
He was the new covenant.
A new light for darkness.
A tree whose fruit never withers.

In the quiet rain, whistling wind and roaring thunder
He beckons us.

SOMEONE HAS TO PAY

She spoke of an experience in which no eight-year-old should have had to live through. My eyes misted over as she spoke of living with a step father who had repeatedly molested and raped her from the time she was a little girl. Her step father had threatened to kill her sisters and her mother if she ever told. This woman was so beautiful physically. However, I'm sure she didn't know it because she wore dark sunglasses all the time. I met her during one of my college classes. I never saw her again after that quarter. I hope she was able to overcome what had happened to her.

"According to the U.S. Department of Justice, an estimated 91% of the victims of rape and sexual assault are female."

SOMEONE HAS TO PAY

He caused her so much pain
The early years were abysmally insane
With a free display of artificial joy
Never to fully enjoy playing with a toy or a boy.

That day he laughed at her humiliation
Taunting and teasing her slow disintegration
From year to year and shame to shame
Too naive, too dishonored to tell Mom his name.

When his evil eyes met hers, she would cringe
Later anger could knock a door from the hinge
His life appeared to be normal anyway
As he denied the memory of that rainy, dark day.

Anger, intense and deep kept friends at bay
Fear and anxiety mounted each passing day
She kept everyone at arms length
As deep depression covered her soul like a tent.

Telling a friend would set her free
To find that her bitterness was once nailed to a tree
So much life missed, so much of her hidden
Sprang forth as she told the forbidden.

Years later, his still, cold body laid
The past debt was finally paid
No more strong bars, no more smelly cages
No more fear, no more rage.

Women Admired

Jackie Kennedy and Marilyn Monroe were two women I admired in my youth. There weren't any Black women that were perceived as newsworthy. These two women caught my eye. Jackie was simply beautiful. She was smart and she demonstrated such strength, resolve and class when President Kennedy was assassinated. Marilyn Monroe was beautiful and glamorous. Just what every young girl wants to be. As I became a woman, I discovered Maya Angelou's talent and strength, because of my love of poetry. Mother Teresa was the demonstration of love and simplicity. Oprah Winfrey is one awesome woman. I'm glad that my nieces have the opportunity to experience such a successful, high profile and touchable celebrity in their lifetime.

Another woman to be admired is current Secretary of State, Condoleezza Rice.

WOMEN ADMIRED

Maya Angelou queen of prose, a caged bird
Of struggle, but still she rose.

Jacqueline Kennedy was a White House class act.
With a famous, philandering mate named Jack.

Marilyn Monroe was loved by all men.
While Norma Jean was never happy within.

Sweet Mother Teresa loved all manner of men
She taught that to "love not" was the greatest sin.

Oprah Winfrey, one "bad" talk show hostess
Where ever she goes, Here! Here! She's toasted!

Five great women we treasure and love
Choice, appointed maidens inspired by the dove.

A Pause From The World

preacher once told me that God is omnipresent. He indicated that He was everywhere at the same time. He is also the wind, the sunlight and the rain.

He's with us always, even unto the end of our time.

Pause From The World

Walking in the woods with Him
Mesmerized by His beauty and serenity
Even the leaves lie prostrate before Him
Secretly praising Him beneath my feet
Others, like seraphim, watch me from above
The aroma of the forest engulfs me
While the intermittent noise of
His beautiful creation passes by,
Their faces in awe of His presence.

Everyday I think of His majesty
His glance is a warm ray of sun.
The memory of His hand on mine.
My private reflection about Him
Is my pause from the world.

SEPTEMBER 11, 2001:
WAR ON AMERICA

On September 11, 2001, terrorists invaded the borders of the United States. Airplanes carrying human cargo, piloted by the enemy on a suicide mission, struck the World Trade Center and The Pentagon. The world watched as 5,000 Americans lost their lives. Martin Luther King said in one of his famous speeches, that America must reap past violence that it sowed. Was 9/11, the beginning of the fulfillment of that prophecy?

> *"There will be wars and rumors of wars.*
> *However, the end is not yet."*

SEPTEMBER 11, 2001: WAR ON AMERICA

If the people would seek his face;
The pain and suffering He could erase.

If the people would know their place
With swiftness to their side He'd haste.

When the people release their faith,
The crooked places are made straight.

Once again truly love their neighbor
Helping the fatherless and the lonely widow.

Forget the color of their many tones of skin;
See His spirit that lives deep within.

Loose the boast and evil pride of life,
And thank Him for blessings, favor and light.

For the kingdom of God is at hand;
A phenomenon within the heart of man.

An earth filled with love, joy, and peace,
Once His awesome kingdom is released.

The kingdoms of this present world
Can become the kingdom of God.

It starts in every heart of man;
Seeking the Lord, so He will heal our land.

THE GOD CHILD

Ronie Renae Spencer was born on February 25, 2000. She is a very joyful and an amazing child. She is wise beyond her years. At three years of age, she speaks of Jesus returning to earth. She hums to the tune of "This Little Light of Mine" as she plays with her toys. In church service, she loses herself in praise and worship. Later on, you find her in front of her television enjoying her cartoons: *Dora, the Explorer* and *Spongebob Squarepants*.

"Every child is a diamond…"
Mary McLeod Bethune

THE GOD CHILD

After the long, painful drive
Her entrance confirmed a Mother's dream.
The sack kept her fed, warm and alive
Incubation would never end, it seemed.

A birthday brought joy and smiles
God's future, righteous judge
Cars and buses travel many miles
To gaze upon the skin of sweet fudge.

A great delight to Mom and Dad
The smile that lights their world
She was the daughter they never had
A crowned head of anointed curls.

Whose child is this?
Parents, God Parents, who knows.
She appears on every Christmas list.
For gifts, clothes and pretty hair bows.

In days to come, she'll wear jewelry of gold
Among great men, she'll take her seat
Conversation sprinkled with wisdom and odes
And divine protection beneath her feet.

THE PROPHETESS

When Jesus ascended to heaven, he left gifts among men. They were the apostle, prophet, evangelist, pastor and teacher. These gifts walk among us and you know them by their fruit. They are acknowledged in the church and disguised in the workplace.

"Where talent and passion crosses, therein lies your calling." Aristotle

THE PROPHETESS

From the womb she is called
Incubated within a tissue wall
Growing in confidence to stand tall
An oracle to the nation, God's awaited gift.

A gift of knowledge to give heavenly tips
Of healing balm from anointed lips
Most will come for a single sip
Of a much-needed word from the Lord.

Sometimes His word will be hard
Though every ear gives great regard
To admonishments that are familiar or odd
For keeping their hearts in all its ways.

Her costly anointing from the ancient of days
Comes from the way she lives and prays
She must surrender to know his ways
She'll give up her sacred right and
Set sail by his guiding light
That chases away the day from the night.

HOSANNA! HOSANNA!

Many years ago in a little town called Bethlehem, a child was born. It was prophesied before his conception that he would be great. And He is.

Jesus is the reason for the season.

HOSANNA! HOSANNA!

Hosanna, Hosanna
Bright, shining star
Help us in the midst of war.
Up above the heavens so bright
Interceding through the night.
Hosanna, Hosanna
Grandest, solitary star.
The world will soon
Know who you are.

THE READY CHURCH

*T*he songwriter sings, "Get right church and let's go home." Christians are in preparation and look forward to the day that He will split the eastern sky. Biblical historians proclaim that every eye will be able to see Him. And in the twinkling of an eye, we'll all be "caught up"—and forever to be with the Lord.

A church is a person or a community.

THE READY CHURCH

Red, yellow, black and white
All shapes and sizes in His sight.

From Senegal to a U.S. Mall
He intercedes for them all.

Every knee must bow and
Every tongue must confess
To enter His eternal rest.

Forgetting previous goals and dreams
Listening for His song to sing.

His house of many fine mansions
Requires neither change or expansion.

As the kingdom begins to rise and twinkle.
Eliminating all human spot and wrinkle.

A mind stayed on him has great peace
A temple that lacks the mortal's disease.

Lose nothing that He will not return a hundredfold.
He blesses your life with streets of gold.

THE MIRACLE SURGEON

*D*octors had tried everything. I had changed my diet. I tried alternative cures. I had tried several drugs. My doctors told me that we had exhausted all of our options. I was surfing the net and met Dr. Toaff on the information highway. I sent him an e-mail and he quickly telephoned me. He indicated that the procedure he would use was an inspiration from God. That caught my attention, of course. He was unlike any doctors I'd met. He surprised me with his genuine concern and upstanding bedside manner. With much fear and trepidation, I finally scheduled the surgery. The rest of the story is history. Dr. Toaff, you're the greatest!

Don't just stop at a second opinion,
it may take a third one
to reach your health goal.

THE MIRACLE SURGEON

Down a long, winding hallway

He pushed the bed himself

Jokes scattered with chants to his God

The smell of bleach as we traveled

The cool Alaskan corridor

With absence of deadly, black germs

Another feet of distance and a turn

That would change the essence of life

The light above was bright

It was not the tunnel of death

Each nurse was joyfully kind

The medicine man kept a check on pain

There was laughter, jesting

Assurance in Him who would guide the scapel

With a smile and a wink, a lengthy deep sleep

Eyes opened wide to a new world

No memory or grief for the previous

The painful part is escorted away

And turned a frown upside down.

ORDER FORM

☐ Please send me _____ copies of Pearls from the Soul at $14.95. Add $3.50 for U.S. shipping. Allow 15 days for delivery.

(Call for information on volume order discounts cost for Canadian/International shipping)

☐ Check or money order for $ _____ is enclosed.

☐ Please charge my: ☐ Visa   ☐ MasterCard   ☐ American Express

Card # _____

Expiration Date _____

Credit Card Billing Address _____

City _____ State _____ Zip_____

Signature _____

☐ Shipping Address

Name_____

Address _____

City _____ State _____ Zip _____

Telephone _____ Fax _____

Email _____

Mail or Fax a copy of this order form to:

    Dante's Publishing
    P.O. Box 39
    Lovejoy, GA 30250-0039
    Phone: (678) 479-1216
    Fax: 770 473-9225
    Email: mrenae@bellsouth.net
    Web: www.pearlsfromthesoul.com